For you, as you go on a new adventure
walking through this book.
—M. B.

First published in the United States of America in 2021 by Chronicle Books LLC.
Originally published in Slovenia in 2018 by Miš Publishing.

Library of Congress Cataloging-in-Publication Data available.

ISBN 978-1-7972-0792-6

Manufactured in China.

Design by Riza Cruz.
Typeset in True North and Brandon Grotesque.
The illustrations in this book were rendered in pencil,
ink, acrylic, and watercolor.

10 9 8 7 6 5 4 3

Chronicle Books LLC
680 Second Street
San Francisco, California 94107

Chronicle Books—we see things differently.
Become part of our community at www.chroniclekids.com.

EVERY LITTLE KINDNESS

MARTA BARTOLJ

chronicle books · san francisco

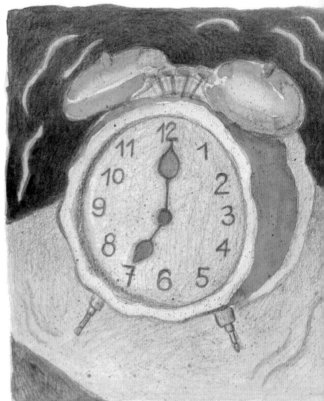

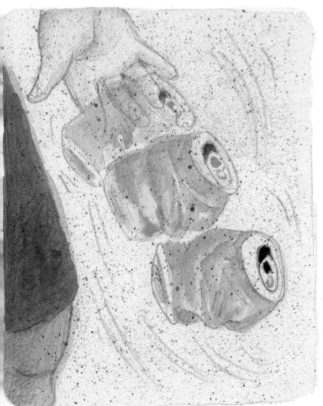